a book with no name

Ken Edwards

a book with no name

Shearsman Books

First published in the United Kingdom in 2016 by
Shearsman Books
50 Westons Hill Drive
Emersons Green
BRISTOL
BS16 7DF

www.shearsman.com

ISBN 978-1-84861-500-7

ACKNOWLEDGEMENTS
'Frequently asked questions', 'Dialectics', 'It', 'Nobody there', 'Fall',
'Persons' appeared in *Golden Handcuffs Review*.
'Equivalence', 'Text', 'Thing', 'History of a thought', 'Be', 'Breathe',
'Love story' appeared online at *Intercapillary Space*.
'Belief', 'Who do you think you are', 'A death in the family'
appeared in *Litmus Magazine*.
'Water', 'Live at Birdland', 'Animals have no names', 'Where are the
animals going' appeared in *PN Review*.
'Infinity' appeared in *Unthology* 7.
'It', 'Like', 'Threat', 'Dialectics' appeared online at kenedwards.eu

Thanks to the editors involved: Lou Rowan, Michael Peverett,
Dorothy Lehane & Elinor Cleghorn, Michael Schmidt,
and Ashley Stokes & Robin Jones.

Thanks to Brian Marley and Lou Rowan
for help, advice and encouragement.

Contents

one

two

three

coda

for Elaine, as ever

If the fool would persist in his folly he would become wise.

Blake, *The Marriage of Heaven and Hell*

one

Beginning

In the beginning there was nothing. And nothing moved nothing was moving. Nothing moved. Nothing was moving it was moving but at first it wasn't going anywhere. Nothing was moving but how? There wasn't anything there to move. How can nothing move? But you could say nothing was moving moving out of nothing it was moving out of nothing into a new space which had come out of nothing. Nothing had been born and there it was. How can nothing be but there it was. It was and is. That is to say it came from something else which was nothing which was before and which was nothing before. It was there and is there and it had come from what was before which was nothing. Before all this there was nothing it wasn't going anywhere because there wasn't anywhere for it to go. That was before and this is after. After is different it is somewhere and it is possible to move to it because there is somewhere for movement to happen and movement can happen there is movement and it moves. Now there is movement. Everything is movement everything fluctuates there is movement everywhere you can say that everything moves it has moved out of nothing. There are fluctuations and there are ripples everything ripples. You can see the ripples but also you are the ripples because the ripples are everything. You are rippling you are moving you are in movement but you don't know where you're moving to because this is all there is so there is nowhere else to move to until you move to it and then it becomes where you have moved to and you can see it it is here and it is you. You are here but you don't know where you've come from you have come from nothing and you don't know nothing you can't imagine nothing even though that's what you have come out of. And you are rippling and moving and the movement is you. And there is movement and fluctuation and the movement is not you or at any rate there is movement which seems not to be you. The sun is moving across the sky and the birds move across the sky and the fish are rippling in the water and the train rumbles along the track and a song comes on the radio and the window rattles and somebody is shouting to a child and there you are you are trying to understand. You are trying to understand are you you how are you you you came out of nothing how are you here? And it becomes even more mysterious.

Dance

When the light comes it all starts. It comes in fits and starts. It comes in colours. When the light comes on they start they come on in colours. They start to move the colours start to move they move more quickly. More and more quickly they move at first in fits and starts and then continuously the colours moving and changing places continuously and continually and it all comes together soon pretty soon it all comes together. The light shows the movement. It moves at the speed of thought and together they all move and move until they reach the speed of thought. They are as one. They are one. They are one and then they are two. They are two and then they are three they move at the speed of thought. The two are black and the three is white. They are three and then they are four they are joined by a fourth and then by a fifth and a sixth. There are six in all. Two are black and three are white and the other one is like the sun. They move and ripple and dance it's a dance the fish are dancing they dance in the water the black and the white and the sunlike one dancing at first in fits and starts and then continuously until they reach the speed of thought they are like thoughts in the way they speed all together the dance is their thinking they think continually they think therefore they dance. This is a thought that they are thinking that they must dance. The three white together and the two black together and the sunlike one alone. Then one of the white goes with one of the black and the second of the white goes with the sunlike one. And the other black goes with the third of the white. And the sunlike one goes with the first white and the second white goes with the third white and the other black goes with the first black. And then the first white with the other black the second white with the first black and the third white with the sunlike one. And so the other black with the second white and sunlike with the first black and the third white with the first white. But the first white goes with the second white and the first black with the third white and sunlike with the other black. And then the third white joins the other two white and the other black joins the first black and sunlike is alone again. That's how it all comes together and falls apart. After that it starts over again but in a different sequence it doesn't repeat. There is never exact repetition. That's how it all comes together and falls apart continually it's what we call thought it happens at the speed of thought. The fish ripple the water ripples they are moving through the water and the water is moving through them they move through the light and the light moves through them they are the light they seem to move without thought because they are at the speed of thought which is the only constant in the dance which is like a dream which is like a dream of thought which is thinking without end without end in sight at first in fits and starts and fits and starts and then continuously and continually and it seems without end when you think about it.

Belief

I believe there's something. I believe there's something there. I believe there's something in it. Something in it that is there. There is there. Here is here and there is there. Up there is there and down here is here and that's how it is. I believe in how it is. I believe you can see that. If you can't see it it may be because it isn't there or it may be that it is there and you just can't see it. So you have to believe it. If you can see it it's there and if you can't see it you just have to believe it's there. Something or someone. If there's someone you can talk to them. You have to have someone to talk to. Everybody has to have someone to talk to. If there was no-one you'd be talking to yourself which doesn't make any sense. It wouldn't make any sense at all. So you see there must be someone. Someone is talking someone must be listening. Talking is happening which is the movement of sound waves in the air which is the lips moving you can see the lips moving. Because of the light waves because there is the light. Where do the light and sound waves come from they don't come out of nothing. They are all the same thing. The thing is that if it came out of nothing it wouldn't make any sense and it does make sense. So it is a thing and it exists and it will go on existing and they say nothing lasts forever so they say one day it won't exist any more but where will it go then? Where will the thing go that has existed? It has to go somewhere. And if it is somewhere it's there. Will it come back or will it be another thing? It's a question of whether you believe what they say. What will the new thing be will it be the same as the old thing and if it is the same will it actually then be the old thing or as good as? It has to make some kind of sense because the talking continues and if it didn't make any sense then there wouldn't be any point in the talking or the writing or the telling but there is a point because it continues the sound patterns and the lips and the fingers moving and people seem to understand it. So there's something in it. That's what it comes down to and it doesn't finish just because they say nothing lasts forever. What do they know anyway? That's what it comes down to. There's got to be something in it. That's how it is. I mean it makes sense.

Nowhere

You what? You saw what? You don't know what. You're talking. You're just talking. You're talking and you're talking. You don't know what you're talking about. You're talking about what you saw. What did you see? They say what you see is what you get. So is what you get what you see? If you see it you've got it or else you've got to get it. Is that it? Have you got that? Where were you? Where are you now? You don't get it. Can't you see? Is what you get what you see or else is what you see what you get? Is that what you're saying? You say you have been there. Where is that? You've seen it. You have just been there. You've been talking about it for all this time. You've talked about it and now you have been. You talked and talked about it and now you have been there. You have been and you've talked about it but you don't get it. You still don't get it. You have been where you were going and you got to do that. After all this time at least you got to do that. And it wasn't much. You got to do that and it wasn't much not at all. You got there finally. It wasn't much to write home about. You were talking about it but it wasn't much in the end to write home about. So you came home? Did you come home? What did you see? There wasn't much there. There wasn't much to see. But now you've been there. At least you've been there. Now you can talk about it. After all this time you can talk about it. After all this time. What was it like? It was much like anywhere else. Was it worth going or wasn't it? It was nowhere much. It was nowhere. What will you do about it now? You don't know what you'll do. Did you really get there? How did you get there? Was it really there? Where? There wasn't any there. Was there? It was there and then it wasn't there any more. At least it would have been an experience. Did you come back? Or are you still there? Was it an experience? You still have the experience you see if it was an experience. You see? You say you didn't come back. You went there but you didn't come back so you're still there. You must still be there. How will you get back? How will you get back home? Where is that? Can you see? Can you talk about it? Why talk about it no point in talking about it. No point at all. It's just there. It's nowhere. It's nowhere much. You got nowhere. But at least you can call it home. You can call it home even if it isn't home. You can talk about it and call it home. You went there and back. No you didn't you went there and you never came back. Where is back? Nowhere. Where is home? Home is nowhere. You didn't come back so you're still there but you're here. You're still here. You're here not there. But you got to talk about it even though you don't know what you're talking about. It's all about where you went and where you got to and how you got there and whether you came back it's not clear. Where you went is nowhere. Where it was is not clear. You went nowhere. Now where are you going? Now you're still going nowhere. You're going nowhere and you're talking about it. You see? You think you don't know where you are but you're right there. Or in other words you're right here. You're talking about here in other words. That's right. You're right here in the middle of it. You're right in the middle that's where you are. In other words you were right in the middle all this time and you're still there. It's nowhere. This is where you are. It's nowhere and you're right in the middle of it.

Nobody there

Is anybody there? Is anybody there? Is there anybody there? There's nobody there. Is anybody there? No there's nobody. Nobody there. There must be somebody. There must be somebody there. Is there anybody? No there's nobody there. There's nobody. That can't be right. There must be somebody. Somebody must be there. Is there? There must be. There must be somebody there. It can't be right that there's nobody there. Is anybody there? What's the matter? Is there nobody there? There used to be somebody there. Now there's nobody. There's nobody there that's what the matter is. There was always somebody there. Was there? Was there always somebody? There may have been somebody but now there's nobody. Something must be the matter there's nobody there now. Somebody used to be there. There was somebody. There always used to be somebody. Somebody was always there. Somebody was there and nothing was the matter. Nothing used to be the matter. Nothing was the matter when there was somebody there but now nobody is there so something must be the matter. Something must be the matter because there's nobody there. What is the matter now? Is somebody there now no there's nobody there. There used to be somebody. Now there's nobody. Nobody's there but somebody used to be. Something must be the matter. Is anything the matter? What is the matter? What is the matter something must be the matter. It seems there's nobody there that is what seems to be the matter. That can't be right. Somebody must be there.

Infinity

There's a room and then there's a little room and another little room off that. And then a room and a room and more rooms and then a room. And beyond that is a little room and then a large room and a room. And in through there there's another and beyond another and a room beyond. And from here they go into another room and that's the little room right there. And then the main room. The room where it happens and the room where they prepare for it to happen and the room where they go after. Then there's a room off that and a room off that and off that and off that and off that. That's where it all goes on where they go that's the room or if not the room then the room beyond that that's where it all happens and after it happens there's another room where they go. And they all gather in that room and they talk and remark upon the room whether it's a good room or not and they remember another room was that as good a room as the room that is the room they're in or wasn't it perhaps it wasn't or perhaps it was another room they were thinking of. Perhaps they mistook that room for that room. That's the room they go into and that's the room they don't. The room they don't is still there it's locked you can't go in there unless you get a key but to do that you have to visit another room and another room and then beyond is the room where you get the key but then you have to find your way back through the first room and the second room and the third room and the fourth room so it may not be worth it. It may not be worth entering the room because there are other rooms that are just as good just as worth entering where you can do what you need to do where you can spend as much time as you like. And when you've finished you can go into the next room that's what they do go into the next room and gather there before going into the room beyond. And the room you go into before the room in which whatever happens happens is called the green room and the room you go into after is called the white room so you can easily identify it and not confuse it with the red room the blue room the yellow room the black room or the room of many colours. But the room of many colours leads into the black room and that leads to the yellow room which leads to the blue room which leads to the red room which leads to the white room and then you're back in the green room. That's where everybody goes. They go into that room and they stay there for a while and if you ask for the toilet they tell you it's beyond the next room just go left and left again and that room is the toilet and you can go to the toilet. That little room is the toilet. You can go there. Everybody goes there. And off the toilet is another toilet and then another toilet and so there are plenty of toilets in fact an infinite number of toilets so they estimate everybody can go to the toilet and everybody does. And everybody goes. Everybody is going. And when you've finished don't forget to wash your hands and then you can join everybody in the next room which is the room everybody goes to. You go right and right again to reach that room. You can't miss it. It's quite a large room. And inside that room is another room and within that an inner room which nobody really knows about but is a room that has been rumoured. The rumours spread all around the room and spill over into the adjoining rooms and then the rooms beyond that where everybody has gathered. That's where the rumours go and they go on forever. That room is locked. Is it the same room or a completely different one? Nobody can say. Nobody knows what's happening in that room but they wait in the rooms where they are or where they are urged to gather and pass the time talking and waiting until further notice for further information.

Frequently asked questions

Would you like to come this way? Would you like to sit down? Do you know where you are? Do you know why you are here? Would you like something to drink? Why not? Do you know your rights? Can you please focus your attention? Can you answer the question? What was that? What was that you said? Why did you say that? What was that about? You don't know? Can't you remember? When was it? Can you give more detail? Where were you? What happened? Was that what was supposed to happen? What was supposed to happen? Did it? What are you doing? Where are you going now? What are you up to? What's that? When? What do you mean? You don't know? What was that again? Where? With what? So what exactly happened? Can you cast your mind back? What were you doing? With whom? How did it happen? What happened next? How did that come about? What did you think about it? Did you even think about it? Do you even think when things like that happen? Are there any thoughts going through your mind and if so what? What does that mean? What do you mean by that? So what do you expect? Why do you say that? What was that? Can you answer in more detail? Can you add any more? Do you expect us to believe that? Do you expect us to believe anything you say? Can you speak up please? Are you having us on? What do you mean you don't know? How can you not know? If that's what you meant why didn't you say so? Why did you make that statement? Would you like to retract that statement? Do you regret saying that? Why not? Was what you said true? Can you please answer? Why did you lie? Did you even think of the consequences? What are you thinking now? Is there anything at all going through your head? If the question was put to you in a different way would your answer be different? Why do you say that? Can you say more? What do you expect anyone to believe? Is that so? How can you justify that? Can you please speak in English? How do you expect people to understand you? Would you like to think about it? Would you like more time? Would you like more time to think about it? Why not? Can you please compose yourself? Do you think the world owes you a living? Is that right? Why do you say it's unfair? Did you ever think about fairness when all this was happening? What do you mean by that? Is there any point in saying that? So why did you say it? Are you saying that's not what you said? So what did you say? Can you explain? Do you know what the consequences will be? Do you know what is likely to happen next? Have you given this any thought? Have you given any thought to the gravity of your situation? Would you like to reflect on this? Have you anything more to say? Do you realise this is your last chance? Is there anything more you would like to add?

Dialectics

This. This is. This is not. This is this is this is not. This is this is this is not the way. This is not the way. This is the way. This way this is not the way. This is not the way not the way. Not the way this is not the way. Not the way it was. This is not the way it was. This is not the way it was not the way it was. It was not the way it was. It was not the way it was not. The way it was was not the way. The way it was was not the way supposed. The way it was was not the way this is not the way. It was not supposed. It was not supposed to be the way. It was not the way supposed. It was not supposed to be this way. The way it was is not the way it was supposed. This is the way it was not supposed. This way was not supposed this is not the way it was supposed. This is not the way it was supposed. Not the way it was supposed to happen. This is the way it was not supposed to happen. This is not the way it was supposed to happen not the way it was supposed to happen. It was not supposed to happen this way. It was not supposed to happen this way it was not supposed to happen. It was not supposed to happen. This is not the way it was supposed to happen.

It

It is this. It is. Or is it? It may be. But then again it may not. It can't be determined. Could it? No it couldn't. We can't determine whether it is. Or what it is. It isn't possible to do so. We can speculate about it. We can make assertions about it. We can construct narratives about it. But it's not possible to do much more. That's what it comes down to. It comes down to not much more than that. And that's about it. So it's time to look outside. What is it doing? It's raining. This is it.

Persons

I am saying this this is what I am saying. I am saying this I said it before but you disagreed. You said this was not what you said you said you disagreed with what I said. You disagreed with what I said you said. You said that what you were saying was something quite different but I said that's not what I said. What I said was this and I have said it before on many occasions in fact you heard me say it but you disagreed with me when I said this you said something quite different. I can see what you're saying but what I am saying is this. What you are saying is something quite different and I can see that this is something you are saying and that you have said it before but this is not what I am saying. This is not what I said. What I said was something quite different from what you said and I disagree with you about what you said I said. You said that what you said was different from what you said before and I said that I agreed with you. I agreed that what you said was different. But you are saying that I disagreed with you about what I said before and I did not disagree with you I did not disagree with you at all but I said that what I said was what I said and that's what I am saying. And you said that you agreed with me but what you are saying is different from what I said before on previous occasions and I agree with you on this. I agree with you about this and I am not saying that. I am not saying that at all. If I said this once I said it many times and you agree with me about this that I have said it many times and on many previous occasions. And you said that he said it too and I agreed with you that he did say this too. He said it before and you heard him say it. I heard him say it. He said it to me and he said it to you and he said the same thing on each occasion and I agreed with him when he said it but you said you disagreed. He says that he has spoken to you and you said you disagreed with what he said about what I said and what I said you had said. I have spoken to him and I said to him that I had spoken to you and that you and I had agreed what to say and that there was no more to be said. But he says he is not in agreement with this he agrees with some of what I said and with some of what you said but he does not agree with what both you and I agreed on. What he is saying is something quite different and he has said it before and will say it again but it is something quite different from what you and I previously agreed and what we now agree about. He says he will speak to you and to me and he will also speak to her because she has something to say about it too but we don't know what that is. I have heard her say something about this and I am not sure whether she agrees with him or whether what she is saying is in agreement with either you or me or with what you and I have agreed. What I am saying is that she may disagree with him or she may agree with him and she may disagree with what I said or with what you said or she may agree with both you and me. If she agrees with him or with you or with me or with all three then I agree that it should be as agreed and what I said before should stand but if she disagrees with him or with you or with me or with all three we shall all have to speak together and come to some agreement. And if we cannot come to an agreement then we shall have to agree to differ.

No such thing as repetition

No such thing as repetition. No such thing as repetition there is no such thing as repetition. There is no such thing as repetition. Because. Because when a thing happens. Because when a thing happens for the first time it has not already happened. It has not already happened. It has not already happened when a thing happens for the first time. It has not already happened and when it happens again. When it happens again. And when it happens again it has happened before. There is no such thing as repetition because when a thing happens for the first time it has not already happened. And when it happens again and when it happens again it has happened before. It has happened before. And when it happens again it has happened before so inevitably. It has happened before so it has happened before so inevitably at once. So inevitably at once. So inevitably at once there is a difference. There is a difference. At once there is a difference. There is no such thing as repetition because when a thing happens for the first time it has not already happened and when it happens again it has happened before so inevitably at once there is a difference.

Changes

Everything's changing. It's changing. It's changing all the time. Everything's changing everything's changing but it's still the same. Everything's changing all the time everything's changing all the time but it's still the same. But it's still the same it stays the same it still stays the same. It changes it changes it changes it stays the same. It stays the same it's still the same but then it changes then it changes everything changes. The things that stay the same then start to change they start to change they change they change all the time they change they are changing. They change and change but then everything's the same. Everything's the same all the time it's all the same it's all the same all the time and then it changes. There are changes happening they're happening all the time. Changes are happening all the time all the time they're happening all the time changes are happening and still it's all the same. Still the same thing is happening. Still the same still the same every time the same the same thing happening the same thing happening all the time it's still the same it's all the same it's all the same all the time it stays the same all the time it's still the same it's still the same and then it changes. And then it changes it changes again it's starting to change everything changes everything is changing it's changing all the time it is changing and changing the changes are happening they are starting to happen all the time there are changes happening all the time and yet it's still the same. It makes no difference it's still the same. It starts to make a difference it starts to change there are changes happening but the same things are happening it's all the same there is no difference. People say there is no difference it makes no difference to them. People say it makes no difference it's all the same. They say it's all the same to them. People say if it's all the same to you it's all the same to me it makes no difference. People say the changes are all the same they're all the same changes and so it makes no difference if it changes because it stays the same. It's all the same to me they say it makes no difference. It makes no difference to me. There's no difference in the way it changes it just changes and changes but it's all the same to you and it's all the same to me. And yet it's changing you can see it's changing it can't stay the same it can't it's got to change things can't stay the same all the time there has to be a difference things have got to make a difference that's what they say it couldn't stay the same things are changing all the time they have got to change there are always changes happening all the time it's always been the same things have always been the same that is to say they're always changing they can't stay the same all the time because changes are always happening people say that they have always said that things have got to change they say they are always saying that things have got to change.

Up and down

There. Up there. He's up there. Can you see? Up there. Up there he's up there. Can you see him? Can you? There? That's him. That's him all right. What's he doing? What's he doing up there? What is he doing? He's got up there. He's managed to get up there. There he is. He's there all right. Is he all right? What's he doing there? He must be crazy. What's he going to do? He's crazy. Did you see him? Did you see him get up there? How did he get up there? How did he manage to get up there? It's crazy. How could he? What's he doing now? He isn't? Is he? He isn't going to? Oh my god. What's going on? What's going on up there? Can you see anything? There he is now. He's there he's up there. He's still up there. He's moving I think he's moving. He's moving can you see him? He can't stay up there. Can somebody do something? What's to be done? What can be done can anybody do anything? Isn't there anything that can be done? What's he doing now? There he goes. There he goes now he must be crazy. He's holding on. He can't hold on. He can't hold on much longer something has got to be done. He's still holding on up there it's crazy. He hasn't got long. He's got to come down. How will he come down? He's been up there too long he has to come down. Is he coming down? Oh my god he's coming down. Oh my god. No he's still there he's still there. He's coming down. Can you see he's coming down. He's coming down oh my god. This is crazy. Look he's coming down. Look. Look he's about to come down. Is he coming down yes he is he's coming down. He has got to come down. He's coming down here he comes. Oh my god look. Here he comes here he comes. He's down is he? No he's still there but he's going to come down. Yes here he comes. He's coming down he's coming down he's coming down. Oh my god he's coming down. He's down is he down? Is he down? Can you see? There he goes. He's down he's down. He's down.

Fall

We find ourselves falling. And we try to pick ourselves up but pretty soon we're falling again. Everybody around is falling. As far as we can see there are people falling. Each falls in his or her very personal fashion. Some fall elegantly but for others there is a lot to learn. There remains a great deal to be desired in the manner of falling of certain of us. We hear a great deal of criticism of this even as we are falling. Some lose all their dignity as they fall shouting and screaming and flailing their limbs while others preserve theirs and do not cause such embarrassment. We hear the conversations as we pass. We are passing each other as we fall at different rates in our different manners some faster some more slowly some with grace and style others merely plummeting. Some have a need to maintain decorum others argue that such vain attempts are simply foolish since we are all on the way down and there is nothing to be done about it. Yet others attempt remedial procedures for example constructing parachutes improvised from scarves and pocket handkerchiefs stitched together and attached to belts and some have limited success in that their fall is temporarily slowed or halted or even reversed in some instances at least for a short time so that there is some amelioration but it rarely lasts because sooner or later the improvised parachutes fail and the rate of fall once again begins to pick up. And some attempt to join hands and at least fall together in a co-ordinated fashion while others have closed their eyes and appear to have retreated into their private internal world as they fall. Some have become reconciled with their falling and seem to be at peace. Some make jokes about falling which are greatly appreciated by those around them if we are to judge from the level of hilarity and so pass the time in this way. And some deny that we are falling at all saying it is a psychological illusion saying that we are all still in the same place and that it is the world that appears from our point of view to be forever receding upwards but that this is of no significance and we should stop worrying about it. Others claim falling is a punishment for past transgressions specifically citing the sin of pride that inevitably precedes a fall and these people appeal constantly for collective repentance and atonement as the only solution to the problem if problem indeed it is and they solicit donations in order to better spread the word but none of this appears to have the desired effect. And so we continue to fall. We continue to fall to the bottom. There is a great deal of speculation and fear about the bottom. There is even panic about what reaching the bottom may mean and about the extreme pain and carnage that may ensue. But this is premature some argue. The bottom could still be some way off. There is no point in speculating and worrying about reaching the bottom until we actually arrive there or until we have some hard evidence that it is approaching and this is not the case. We haven't reached the bottom yet and probably will not for some time. But if or when we do it will at least be a new experience. There is always something to be said for new experiences. Some of those falling say it will be a milestone. That's the buzz around here. Reaching the bottom will be a milestone and so those of us who take that view say that we shall look forward to that. But some say there may be no bottom. They say that if there is no bottom then we shall always fall we shall always be falling without end and that this is our only destiny to be forever falling and it is possible or indeed very likely we shall never reach bottom because the bottom is merely an illusion produced by our minds. Others argue that there must be a bottom because the fall would otherwise be meaningless because the whole idea of a bottom gives purpose and dignity to our falling and we should look forward to and welcome our arrival at the bottom whenever it should happen. And the arguments become quite heated at times on occasion resulting in disgraceful scenes of violence and it seems there is going to be no resolution to this conflict any time soon.

two

Blues

Every day the sun comes up. Every day the sun comes up the sun comes up. The sun comes up every day. It comes up every day. It comes up every day the sun comes up. Every day the sun comes up. Every day the sun comes up but I go down. The sun comes up but I go down. I go down every day the sun comes up. I go down every day you know I go down every day. I go down every day you know she's gone. I know she's gone I know it every day. I know it. She's gone and left me I know it. I know she's gone and left me I know it every day. She's gone and left me and I'm so alone. She's left me and I know I'm so alone I'm so alone every day she's gone. And now she's gone and I'm so alone. You know she's gone and left me you know she's left me so alone. You know I work so hard. You know that you know I work so hard. I work hard every day. I work hard every day from morning till the sun goes down. From morning till the sun goes down I work so hard every day you know I do. You know what I'm talking about. I work so hard every day from morning till the sun goes down that's what I'm talking about. She took my money you know she did. She took my money you know she took all my money. I work so hard she took all my money. She took all my money she went off. She took all my money she went off with someone else. She took all my money she went off with someone else that's what she did. That's what I'm talking about. She took all my money she went off with someone else and now she's gone. She went off with someone else and now she's gone. She went off with all my money she went off with someone else. And now she's gone. She went off and left me all alone. She went off with someone else that's what she did you know what I'm talking about. And now she's gone I'm so alone I'm going to leave this town. I'm going to leave this town that's what I'll do. That's what I'll do I'm going to leave this town I'm getting a train to ride. I believe I'm going to leave this town I'm going to leave this town I'm getting a train to ride. I'm going to leave this town I'm getting a train to ride. I believe I'll go and find her you know I'll find her. Yes I'll go and find her. Yes I'll go and find her I'll get a train to ride. I believe I'll go and find her she's got no place to hide.

Faces

They began to approach slowly from everywhere. Then they were there. Many of them. They crowded around. Some of them appeared to be familiar. Some of them were smiling and nodding. Others had an indeterminate expression you could say a somewhat enigmatic expression. Some of them could be recognised. How could you recognise them? They had features. All were distinguished by features. They could be recognised by their features which were simple and of a familiar pattern. Others were less familiar. Others could not be recognised. Their features were less familiar or completely unfamiliar. They looked like petals of unidentified flowering plants. They resembled flower petals with a skin of moisture on them nodding and smiling or not smiling. There were beads of moisture on them possibly dew. Possibly this was a lingering result of the dew that had accumulated during the night. Possibly there was light rain falling. So many of them. They crowded around in the light rain that may have been falling perhaps in a garden. Perhaps there was a garden and there was light rain falling in it and they were in it. Still they approached and crowded around like flower petals but fewer of them were now recognisable. They could no longer be recognised. Fewer and fewer of them could be recognised. Fewer of them were smiling. Most now had an enigmatic expression. You could say mysterious or unfathomable. It was no longer possible to recognise them and it was no longer possible to say what their expression meant. It was no longer possible to recognise the faces.

Zones

There is a white zone of the province where white people live. They have lived there for generations tending their crops raising their children. And over on the other side live the green people. That is called the green zone. The green people have been there for centuries. From even before there were zones. The white people know nothing of the green people. The green people know everything about the white people all their culture and history and everything because they have read about them in books. The green people hate the white people but dearly want to be like them. The white people have no idea about any of this. The green people have no idea how ignorant the white people really are.

Water

It is a belief. Everybody is entitled to it. It is a belief system it underlies everything but it is undetected. There is all to play for it is entitlement. It plays gently it quenches. It plays and the play of it is endless it is a system. It is a system that quenches itself. But this system is endless. It is energy. It's undetected but it's behind everything. It is hidden. It is behind the walls. It is underground. Sleeping there. It is inside of us can you hear it? The Moon tugs it. Are you listening to it? There it goes again. Listen. It is hidden on the Moon. It really is something. The energy is really something it is something everybody knows. It is something everybody knows but it's unknowable. It is hidden on the Moon and it sublimates on Mars it escapes into deep space. We get it from deep space. We are made of it and we are unknowable. We are moving. Who can know us? It swirls and eddies it takes the form of torrents vortices and whirlpools it has a transcendental element. So salts form in it. And we move with it as we form. It is key to the landscape we say it transcends. It can't be contained. The domes are full of it. The tanks overspill. It is in the pipes. It's in the cesspools gutters drains and pipes but it can't be contained. It's coming through the pipes but the pipes can't contain it any longer. It's coming from upstairs. It's coming down the walls. It's coming down everywhere. Where is it coming from we don't know where it's coming from. It finds its own way. It finds a way it escapes and finds a way it finds a level. It has consequences. It finds its own way down we can't tell the consequences where it all comes down. It soaks muslin and leaves traces. The floor is soaked with it. Absolutely soaked. It leaves damage in its wake. Damage is formed by it. The consequential damage is incalculable. It lashes down without cease it sweeps away villages. It can't be predicted it has no colour. No colour can be observed in it. But it has a cadence. It is profound. Its cadence is profound. It has no colour it has a beautiful translucency with a shimmer in it. Has no colour but what a shimmer. With a shimmer we disappear. We disappear into its profundity into its vast depth we are engulfed and disappear forever. We call it the ocean but it lives in a glass.

Live at Birdland

They sing. They perch. They flit. They preen. They fly. They settle. They hop. They flutter. They walk. They peck. They look. They nod. They flap. They twitter. They call. They threaten. They jump. They mate. They jostle. They stretch. They warble. They nestle. They hover. They glide. They squabble. They feed. They kill. They sleep. They shudder. They fluff. They strut. They display. They sing intermittently. They perch wilfully. They flit threateningly. They preen beautifully. They fly cheekily. They settle prettily. They hop darkly. They flutter brightly. They rarely walk. They peck quickly. They look slowly. They nod purposefully. They flap randomly. They twitter pertly. They call erratically. They threaten firmly. They jump lazily. They mate fitfully. They jostle again. They often stretch. They warble lightly. They nestle loudly. They hover repeatedly. They glide well. They squabble badly. They feed strongly. They kill madly. They sleep nimbly. They almost shudder. They fluff shortly. They strut fearfully. They seldom display. They perch threateningly. They flit beautifully. They preen cheekily. They fly prettily. They settle darkly. They hop brightly. They flutter fearfully. They walk quickly. They never peck. They look purposefully. They nod slowly. They flap badly. They twitter randomly. They call pertly. They threaten erratically. They jump firmly. They mate lazily. They jostle fitfully. They stretch again. They often warble. They nestle lightly. They hover loudly. They glide repeatedly. They squabble well. They never feed. They kill strongly. They sleep madly. They shudder nimbly. They never fluff. They strut shortly. They display intermittently. They sing wilfully. They preen threateningly. They fly beautifully. They settle cheekily. They hop prettily. They flutter darkly. They walk brightly. They peck fearfully. They look quickly. They never nod. They flap slowly. They twitter purposefully. They call badly. They threaten randomly. They jump pertly. They mate erratically. They jostle firmly. They stretch lazily. They warble fitfully. They nestle again. They often hover. They glide lightly. They squabble loudly. They feed repeatedly. They kill well. They sleep strongly. They shudder prettily. They fluff madly. They strut nimbly. They display shortly. They never sing. They never perch. They flit wilfully. They never settle. Hop slowly. Flutter purposefully. Walk badly. Never shudder. They peck wilfully. Fluff threateningly. Strut beautifully. Display cheekily. Look pertly. Never flap. They nod firmly. Twitter lazily. Call fitfully. Never threaten. Never jump. They mate lightly. Jostle loudly. Never stretch. Never warble. Never nestle. They hover strongly. Glide madly. Squabble nimbly. Feed shortly. Never kill. They sing darkly. Never sleep. They perch brightly. Never flit. They preen fearfully. They fly away.

Animals have no names

We hear them at night in the forest but never see them. Their noises come over the water from the outer islands all night long their inexplicable noises. But when the sun comes up they are nowhere to be seen. Nowhere to be seen because they are in hiding. What have they got to hide? We know they are out and about on the islands or in the dark forest in the places nobody goes they are out and about they know we are here but they don't care. They don't care about us. They're out and about in the dark forest and they don't care about us not at all. You can call them all you like they won't answer. They will not answer they just chitter and howl and roar. You may see the prints of their naked feet where they have been. Maybe you can catch their eyes in the dark their eyes glitter. They glitter as they chitter they don't care. They whimper and they bleat they sigh and squeak. We give them names. The Leopard Cat and the mighty Bee. The Naked Mole Rat the Arachnids the Nurse Shark and the Molluscs with their beady eye. These are the names we give them but they have no names. The slovenly Lion the majestic Tapir and many others on land and sea and in the air such as the Humming Bird and indeed birds and bird machines of all kinds how they lurk and shout and perform their mad language games. In the midst of the dark forest they have lost their way. Call out their names all you like they will not answer. They lose their way and blunder in the forest they howl in the mountains but they do not lack confidence at all in any manner whatsoever their confidence is obvious in their stiff-armed strut their simian strategies. They are so sure of themselves. They howl from mountain to mountain. Their terrible soft eyes glitter in the dark. They don't know their names you call them repeatedly but they don't answer. They do not know their names. They have absolutely no idea. They do not answer to their names. They do not appear but you can smell them. The scent tells you they are very close. They are closer than you think. They are magnificent in their way even though they are stupid. They take their terrible revenge they murder their own kind they devour their children. They are crazy they really are. They show no gratitude. They lie and cheat they eat their babies they are stupid. They make war on their own kind with fangs and claws with rockets and swords. They cause explosions. They blunder and shout in the forest and laugh at the moon. They do not care about us. Their throats are warped they have no words they have no names the stupid stupid animals.

Where are the animals going

The animals are running. They are running together. The animals are running away. They are all different sizes. Faint steam rises from their bodies. They are not looking at us. Their eyes are fixed on where they are going. They are fleeing but we do not know what they are fleeing or where they are heading. It is a mystery. Scientists have come up with various possible explanations. The animals appear to be scared you can see it in their eyes. They are scared all right. They are all running together in a group or in several groups. They run and run. Are they trying to tell us something? Nobody knows. Nobody knows what they are trying to tell us.

Threat

The phenomenon has been observed and it is concluded that it poses a significant threat. There can be no certainty about it but there is a widespread perception that this is the case. There are indications of something impending. It is commonly perceived to be a threat. There has been extensive analysis and there can be little doubt. The analysis confirms what has been widely feared for some time. Researchers report that there has been a steady growth in threats such as this over the past year predicted to result in a sharp upturn in the final quarter. Analysts have crunched the data and it is now believed that the threat could increase significantly in the immediate future. Its source cannot be localised. It could arise at any of the cardinal points either within major conurbations or from relatively undeveloped areas. The timeline predicts a number of causes for suspicion and complacency should be avoided. Vigilance must be maintained at all times and at all costs. It is recommended that any complacency should be avoided in the medium and long term as this could result in significant harm. The exact location and nature of the threat are currently the subject of further research but there can be little room for doubt that this is a cause for concern. The findings make an increasingly detailed picture of how current developments in tandem with existing fault lines pose a much more direct threat than we have seen hitherto and there are warnings of sweeping consequences to life and livelihood. An effective threat reduction programme as part of a coherent strategy is recommended although risk analysis suggests that it may already be too late for completely effective and appropriate action in response. The geographical scope of the threat is widening on a daily basis. The situation is deteriorating by the day. A threat intelligence platform that manages the entire life-cycle of threat intelligence from multi-source acquisition to actionable operations across the entire eco-system of existing security devices is recommended but there is no certainty that this would be a viable long-term solution. More research is needed.

The facts

I have the facts. I have those. I have those facts. I have all those facts. I have all the facts. I have those I have. I have examined those. I have examined those facts I have. All those facts I have examined. Those I have. All those I have. All the facts. All those I like. All those. I like those facts. I have all those I like. I have examined all those I like. All those I like I like. All those I have examined. I like those. I have agreed with those. I have agreed with the facts. Those facts I have agreed with. I like those facts I have agreed with. I have examined all those I have agreed I like. I have agreed I have examined those and I like those. I have examined all the facts. I have examined those I like. I have examined all the facts and those I like I have agreed with.

On liberty

They tell us it will be bright. It will chiefly be bright all across the country except for patches of gloom. That's right the gloom will predominate they say. Why do they say this? What right have they to tell us this? What right have they? It's a bloody liberty that's what it is.

They

They say that that's what they say. They say that. They do say that.
That's what they're saying I heard it on the radio. They do say that
that's what they say they say that they do. But do they? But do
they they do. Believe me they do. No but do they? I don't know I
just heard it on the radio that's what they're saying. They said the
same thing yesterday. Did they? Yes they did they said the same
thing yesterday they're always saying that. They've been on about
it before. You don't want to take too much notice of it. They're
always on about it. You don't want to pay too much attention. But
everybody's talking about it they say everybody's talking about it
they say it was on the radio. They're talking about what's going to
happen. What's going to happen? I don't know but they're talking
about it right now. They're talking about it it was in the papers it
was on television it was on the internet it was everywhere what
they were talking about and that's what they're talking about. That's
what they're talking about but nobody knows really. Nobody knows
really they may talk about it but they don't really know. There's a
lot of talk but when it comes down to it they don't know. Don't
they? No they don't they don't know. They really don't know. They
don't know what's going to happen. They don't know what they're
talking about.

Going places

This is all very well but we're not getting anywhere. This isn't getting us anywhere. We're going nowhere with this. What's to be done? We need to be going somewhere. Where can we go? There's a lack of direction. There's a distinct lack of direction not to mention purpose here. Everything points to a lack of purpose. There needs to be some movement. Things need to move. Some people would say things are not moving in the right direction or indeed in any direction. Those people will know where to go. Those people are going somewhere. They have a purpose. You can tell they're going places. They're not just hanging around. You can tell just from their body language. They are here but they won't be sticking around much longer. They are here because they have somewhere to go.

In transit

An hour has gone by. They have already been there for an hour. They are sitting on beige seats. They are in an intermediate state. The colour of the seats is beige and the customers are sitting on them. There are four video screens on the far wall on which images and information are constantly being displayed. The customers wait to hear if their name is called. The customers are getting restless. There are four video screens on the far wall on which images and information are constantly being displayed for the benefit of customers. Ambient music plays very quietly. There is discreet overhead strip lighting. Ambient music has been playing very quietly for an hour. The customers continue to sit. There are low tables. The customers continue to sit on the beige seats while video screens display images and information and ambient music plays very quietly. Mostly they are not looking or appearing to look at the images and mostly not listening or appearing to listen to the ambient music. There are 24 rows of seating. More than an hour has gone by. It is not possible to know whether the images or music are playing in the customers' minds or whether other images or music playing outside of the customers' minds are also playing inside their minds or whether the customers' minds are empty and they are oblivious to the images or music that are playing. It is not possible to see outside. It is not clear what is going on outside. Inside are the customers. Some of them are reading some of them are reading newspapers. It is not clear what is outside. Twelve of them are reading newspapers. It is not clear what they are reading. Eight customers are reading paperback books. Fifteen customers are reading or playing games or listening to music on portable electronic devices. Many customers have bags and sometimes one of them rummages in a bag. The ambient music continues. Some customers are talking among themselves or talking to their children. It is not clear what the customers are saying to each other or to their children or what their children are saying to them or to the other children. They are waiting to hear if their name will be called. The customers are dressed casually they sit on beige seats in front of low tables which are also beige with their bags with them or else on the floor. Metal waste bins are arranged at intervals for the convenience of the customers. Sometimes a customer stands up. While the coloured images continue to change on the video screens and while the music plays discreetly some of the customers walk up and down they just walk up and down for a bit not looking at the screens not paying attention to the music and then they go to sit down again. Their footsteps make no sound on the floor which is grey. The walls are grey. The ambient music stops. The girl says: We are sorry there has been a delay. Will customers please remain seated and wait for further information. The ambient music resumes. Six customers are reading newspapers nine customers are reading paperback books nineteen customers are reading or playing games or listening to music on portable electronic devices. One customer takes a photograph of another customer. Six customers are eating or drinking. Smoking is not permitted. One customer goes to the toilet which is at the other end of the room from the video screens and immediately another customer follows. Three customers are eating or drinking while reading or while playing games on a portable electronic device. The children are getting restless. Crisps snacks and drinks are readily available. Three customers go to the toilet and four customers return from the toilet. Hours go by. This is an intermediate state. The video screens continue and the ambient music continues and the strip lighting overhead continues to illuminate everything the beige seating the beige low tables the grey floor and walls the customers in their different coloured casual clothing their reading material their portable electronic devices their children and their children's toys. The ambient music stops. The girl says: We are very sorry there continues to be a delay. We will have some more information very shortly. Thank you for being patient. The ambient music resumes. One customer takes a photograph. One customer is lying full length on the beige seating perhaps attempting to sleep. Two other customers are asleep on their seats. Another returns from the toilet. Three are grouped together and a fourth takes a photograph of them. A mother takes her child to the toilet. There is no change in the music that is playing and while the coloured images on the screens change all the time they appear to keep returning to the beginning so that then they begin again. Newspapers books and food wrappers are on the low beige tables. Four customers are reading newspapers ten customers are reading paperback books twelve customers are reading or playing games or listening to music on portable electronic devices. Vouchers have been issued to the customers. The vouchers enable customers to purchase a simple meal and a drink. There is no change on the video screens. The customers are starting to get restless and their children too are starting to get restless. They are hoping that their name may be called. Their minds may be filled with images and sounds or their minds may be empty. The vouchers enable customers to purchase a simple meal and a drink but the choice available is limited. This is an intermediate state. The vouchers have been issued as a courtesy to customers. Crisps snacks and drinks can be readily purchased at vending machines adjacent to the waiting area. The girl says: We wish to apologise for the continuing delay but we hope to bring you more information soon. Eight customers are wearing hats. Five have their eyes closed. It may be that their minds are empty. Another customer stands up and goes to the toilet and comes back. Several customers are talking. Four customers are staring at the video screens but not saying anything. The choice available is limited. There is no way of knowing what is going on outside. It is not clear where the outside is or what lies there. One customer has picked up a newspaper that another customer was reading but has now discarded. The outside cannot be accessed at this time. Fifteen customers have their eyes closed fourteen are reading or playing games or listening to music two of those listening to music also having their eyes closed. Children play with toys but are starting to get restless. A limited selection of meals as well as alcoholic and non-alcoholic beverages is available. Discarded snack wrappers and empty drinks cans are crammed into the metal waste bins that are arranged at intervals. They have been there for some hours. The girl says: This is a customer announcement. There is no more information at this time but please bear with us and remain here for the time being until further announcements. A long period has elapsed but no change can be reported. Several customers may be unconscious. Nobody has had their name called but they continue as though they expect this and wait for this. Their minds may be filled or they may be empty. Ambient lighting level has not changed. Ambient sound level has not changed. Colour of seating is beige low tables are beige floor grey walls grey. No customers are reading newspapers four customers are reading paperback books six customers are reading or playing games or listening to music on portable electronic devices. No customers are looking at the video screens. No customer is in the toilet. A day has gone by. The pattern has repeated but there is never an exact repetition there is no repetition the outcome may be different but it is not possible to say what the outcome is. Images on the screens continue ambient music persists. This is an intermediate state. The girl says: This is a customer announcement. Her voice can no longer be heard. There will be a further announcement soon. There are 24 rows of beige seating with low tables in front on a grey floor between grey walls four video screens at one end displaying images and information there are metal waste bins crammed with litter there is ambient music playing and discreet strip lighting overhead. No customers are reading newspapers no customers are reading paperback books no customers are reading or playing games or listening to music on portable electronic devices. Days have gone by. The customers are starting to become restless. They are in an intermediate state. The information on the video screens is meaningless. The girl's voice is indecipherable. Weeks have gone by. Nobody is looking at the video screens. Years go by. They are waiting. They are waiting and waiting. The names will be called soon. They will be called either in order of priority or in alphabetical order. The names will be called one by one. They are waiting to hear their name called.

People

People speak. What people? Common people. Poor people. Naked people. People falling. People sleeping. People went missing. People need people. Who were they? People like you. People stick together. People get ready. People are funny. People are speaking. The dark people. People you know. Very quiet people. How many people? Can't stand people. The common people. Some people are nuns. What are they doing? People speak unknown languages. People are about people. They are people people. Some people are Muslims. People you don't know. What became of them? People huddled in coats. People in the snow. They were good people. All people are people. All people will die. People are very different. People are in a space. What are they all doing? They drive a people carrier. People sigh and they squeak. People are descended from animals. Half the people are drunk. People dress up like people. Some people are doing carpentry. They start to drift away. They think it's all over. These people mean no harm. Where are all the people? There's no accounting for people. There are too many people. How many people are there? People are all the same. People are in the water. People are losing their heads. How could people be so stupid? People are crying for help. Did you see those people? The people of the forest. Where did they end up? People are stuck in the toilet. Some people are on the pitch. They were physically robust little people. People are the fastest animals alive. There's nothing so queer as people. People went into the water tentatively. It was where the people dwelt. People dress up like other people. People fell from the burning buildings. People walked through the empty hospitals. People like that kind of thing. These people are play-acting he said. Do you prefer people or dogs? There are more than ten thousand people. People are being born all the time. Mostly people sat out in the garden. People you wouldn't be seen dead with. Such people are not worth talking to. People just don't know what to do. There are more than a million people. The people united will never be defeated. Was that my people or your people? There were some really nice people there. The dark people mingle with the traffic. People just don't know what's going on. People landed on the moon in 1969. People like to dress up and get drunk. People will tell you all sorts of nonsense. By now the people were slowly drifting away. We never had a problem with those people. These are the last days of the people. There are people and then there are people. How could people be doing this to people? You have to give the people what they want. People were trashing the surrounding villages with malicious persistence. People were getting up to all kind of tricks. What queer little people those were don't you think? On the East Hill people were flying kites. People have got to rely on their common sense. By 2050 there will be nearly 10 billion people. We've got to get these people out of here. People come from miles around to view the lavender fields. Lots of people wondered where the people of colour were. People posted malicious comments on social media which upset people. They're not the kind of people who would do that. People threw themselves from the windows as the fire took hold. People were slipping on the ice and banging onto the pavement. People who need people are the luckiest people in the world. People have the right to do whatever they want provided they. The man in the blue T-shirt was busy talking to people. I'll get my people to call your people is what he said. There were possibly a couple of dozen people as well as children. People will not accept this kind of thing happening to their families. This is a list of people in Hastings in East Sussex in England. Seventy percent of the people who fled to the mountains had not survived. Considering it rained solidly all day a surprising number of people turned up. People were dancing all night and into the early hours of the morning. People are going outside the pub to smoke and drink and cause disturbances. People can be seen in the video acting as if nothing had happened. A crowd of people climbed onto an ancient bus in the dusty heat. The air is filled with the cries of people lost in their dreams. If you knew the half about people you wouldn't know what to think. On the flat sands dotted here and there people were walking their dogs. There were beautiful people moving in the gap between the recycling bins and the waterside. The factory employs 30 people working round the clock in an air-conditioned block without windows. Slowly and inexorably people entered a state of delirium and intoxication of attraction and repulsion. People rolled up the cables and packed up the equipment stacking it neatly in the corners. There has been a great deal of migration recently by the mysterious people from the south. There was a little crowd of a score or so people in the dark up there. Government of the people by the people for the people shall not perish from the earth. Crowds of people had accumulated for the bus that was due to leave at about 8.15. Some people are fixing banners between the trees made of bedsheets with blue writings and drawings on them. Here is the church and here is the steeple here is the priest and here are the people. He replied that he had enjoyed living in Berlin because it was full of crazy people doing meaningless things. We see pictures of black people being led away in handcuffs for not obeying orders to leave their property. By 3.30 the weather got so bad that a memo was sent round the building advising people to go home. The sea was unnaturally calm the sun obscured behind cloud and there were a few people dotted around on the beach. We love the long takes of people walking along grey streets the enigmatic dead whale and the Prince who never appears. To everyone's amazement people were pouring out of their offices all over the neighbourhood to view the eclipse and the churchyard was soon crowded. You know these people some who live alone some with their forearms encased in leather some from the hospital or from over the sea. There were people drinking in the bar but the other people were told they couldn't go in there because it was a private function. A huge lift carried people one floor down to a floor reached otherwise by steps and on the far side by an impossibly raked ramp. People had to produce their tickets and were then led to the room where the film was being shown and they had to watch it. It was really mad stuff with screaming trumpets a guest klezmer clarinetist a tuba solo clattering bongos and bass drum and people dancing in the aisles. Some of the people all of the time or all of the people some of the time but surely not all of the people all of the time? People talked loudly on their mobile phones including a man who described himself as 32 years old and was slagging off his girlfriend for what seemed like hours. He was one of the people who actually appeared in the film with his real wife and friends and the daughter he adopted alongside the actors playing all these people. A few people are trying to continue their lives gathering together what they can wading around fully clothed or paddling in improvised boats or reclining in threadbare sofas on their balconies. People once known once loved are no more but live in the memory of people who have one by one gone and are no more and that's the way it goes. The thought of all those people each with their own tiny task to perform in the vast machinery of killing people and all at risk of being killed themselves is a solemn one. People are coming in and out of the house all the time gathering downstairs talking and laughing and you no longer have any idea who they are or what they are up to. Glittering groups of people are wandering around sipping drinks and sampling canapés in the vast spaces along the wide corridors and hallways up and down spiralling stairs and through offices furnished in gleaming polished hardwood. Thirty people have been identified as dead but the final toll could be more than 120 as many of the bodies may never be recovered because of the intense fire that engulfed the leading carriages. The sea was now slate grey and a stiff breeze was increasingly whipping it up yet small groups of people spaced at wide intervals could still be observed walking slowly and carefully along the front.

Black box

The sun glinted and the customers were peaceful. The sun glinted on the wing. The customers were going nowhere. The sun glinted on the leading edge of the wing of the aircraft on a scheduled flight of a leading airline whose customers were peaceful. On the leading edge of the wing of the aircraft which was a Boeing 777. It took off at 1640 hours the takeoff was uneventful. The sun glinted on the leading edge of the wing of the aircraft on a scheduled flight of a leading airline whose customers were peaceful and going nowhere. There were 239 customers. They were going nowhere. According to satellite and radar evidence the aircraft was flying. It was moving peacefully through the air. The customers watched the sun glint on the leading edge of the wing. But they were going nowhere. The captain of the Boeing 777 communicated with the customers. It was a leading airline. The flight was on schedule. The aircraft continued to fly. The movements were consistent with deliberate action. The aircraft's communications systems including the aircraft and communications addressing and reporting system continued to function. There was no inconsistency. Menu choices included chicken rendang with rice and vegetables and a slice of cake (economy class) and signature satay garlic bread narial chicken with ghee rice mixed vegetables and cashew roll rich bread pudding after dinner mints yogurt (business class). The aircraft's transponder was operating normally. The customers moved peacefully through the air and were communicated with by the captain. The Boeing 777 is a wide body jet aircraft with a seating capacity of 314-451 and a range of up to 9,380 nautical miles (17,372 kilometres). The Boeing 777 flew through the void and continued to fly. It flew through the boundary between airspaces. It continued to fly. Weather conditions were reported to be good. The aircraft possessed a black box flight recorder. The aircraft would have been flying at its cruise speed of 510 knots (945 kph) at an altitude of 35,000 feet (10,700 metres). It was going nowhere. A black box flight recorder was to be found on the aircraft. The captain reported weather conditions were good. The airline crew moved slowly through the cabins to meet the needs of customers. Sunshine glinted on the wing of the aircraft it went like a dream. The black box flight recorder was to be found it was a standard component. The components of the aircraft were all working separately and together. As the aircraft flew through the boundary between airspaces the captain is reported to have said roger that. The aircraft was flying for some hours following its takeoff at 1640 hours. A black box emits ultrasonic signals. At some point the communications systems were switched off. The aircraft flew more than 1,000 miles (1,600 kilometres). The customers' needs were being met. The customers' needs included need for information and were met. At some point the transponder was switched off. The black box was located within the body of the aircraft. A black box is not black. The black box was not black. The airline staff communicated with the customers. They were communicating as the aircraft flew through the void and conditions were reported as normal. The black box could not be communicated with. Black means there can be no communication. Information went into the black box and could not be retrieved. The customers' needs were not being met. Black box means opaque it is a device whose internal workings cannot be known. It can be observed in terms of input output and transfer characteristics but beyond that nothing can be known. The black box was opaque. The black box was a mystery. The black box contained circuitry which was not known. It contained a secret mysterious or complex mechanical or electronic device. The sun glinted on the black box. The components of the aircraft were no longer functioning together. The aircraft was going nowhere. The customers were peaceful. The customers were growing increasingly concerned because their needs were not being met and their information needs were not being met. The customers were going nowhere. The information went into the black box. The information that has been put into the black box should be retrieved from the black box. The black box held all the information. The black box did not return the information. No signals could be obtained from the black box. No information could be obtained from the black box. There was a lack of information and a lack of understanding. The sun glinted on the wing of the aircraft. The black box could not be found. The information could not be found.

three

In or out

There are words and these are they. They reside inside a book. The reader is outside the book. The reader looks at these words that are inside the book. The reader who is outside inspects the inside and sees the words and reads them. Who put the words in the book? Someone must have created the inside that is the content of the book that is within the book and put these words in there that are what the reader is reading now. Was this person on the inside? Was it an inside job? What is outside? Outside is the world and this is where the reader resides. Inside is the book which the reader is outside of. But the book is also inside the world and forms part of it. And now the words of this book have been read and form part of the reader's memory and are inside the reader. These words have somehow got out. Where are they now? What are they doing?

About want

What's it about? What is what about? What was that about? What? That. That? Yes that what was that all about? Who wants to know? People do. What people? People need an explanation. Really? You want to explain it this wants an explanation. There is nothing to explain and that's about it. That is not satisfactory there is something wanting there. Nothing is wanting it's not about anything not about anything in particular. But people want to know. Who are these people? Just people they want to know what it's all about. Why do they want to know? There is something wanting if there's no explanation. There is no explanation it can't be explained. Why not? What is it you want anyway?

Equivalence

Things we thought are not connected can in fact be converted to each other. For example matter is equivalent to energy. And energy can be reduced to the material objects that we desire. Human desire defaults to human error. And error is transformed into an orrery of intricate design. But the orangery that we wander through in delight soon decays to an abandoned lot. And the abandoned place emerges through a series of tunnels and wormholes to become multi-dimensional manifolds. Many of these morph into human shapes shuddering. Those shadowy apes turn into the apex of the heart. And a heartbeat changes subtly to the tapping of a drum through a complex of long corridors. But the corridors lead nowhere they metamorphose into cosmic strings left over from the early universe. Then strings give way to brass that sings aloud. The song is rendered as a series of complex and imaginary numbers. A number substitutes for a name. Your name is called but you do not recognise it and eventually it evolves into random syllables. The phonemes shift to a series of vibrations. This fibrous mass regenerates as the pages of a book. The book has no name and its text which appears to be meaningless transmutes into iconic characters. Cartoon characters hover above a precipice and are transfigured into abstract coloured shapes that dance. The dance is remade as an image woven into a rug. The pattern resolves to a face you recognise. And the face of your loved one takes the nature of an abandoned vessel somewhere on a high ocean.

Like

An ironing board is like the bored teenagers on the promenade. The bored teenagers on the promenade are like hurdlers. Hurdlers are like weightlifters. Weightlifters are like gilded gravel in the bowl. Gilded gravel in the bowl is like an orchestra like a loose dressing-gown cord like sutlers. Sutlers are like guests like merchants under parasols. Merchants under parasols are rucked like a curtain. A curtain is like a bullock a bullock is like shadows that follow the shadows that follow are as smart as a griddle cooling against the wall as smart as the jacks on playing-cards that pop up as if they were dogs. As if they were dogs or like a reader who was half-asleep. A reader who was half-asleep is like Neanderthal Man like footprints over the sandflats. Footprints over the sandflats are like a woman who opens a door and hears music. A woman who opens a door and hears music is sagging like a tired dish. A tired dish is like a tape-recorder like scalded tea-leaves like engravings under tissue paper like a mantelpiece frog like useless chimney stacks like Falstaffian generals. Falstaffian generals are like an exhumed gourd like a breeze like broad sunflowers of empty circumspection like a Welsh rarebit like a bar of light like clockwork like patches from a cycle kit like a tiny English Channel like leaves on the cold sea like a watermark. A watermark is like the smouldering one-off spoor of the yeti. The smouldering one-off spoor of the yeti is sharp as tears. Tears are like soft cheeses like an examination or some vast dinner party or like a melon wedged in a shopping-bag. A melon wedged in a shopping-bag is like lichen. Lichen is like lead. Lead is like an ironing board like the bored teenagers on the promenade.

Likes

Giles Goodland likes Edmund Hardy's photo. Colin Herd likes Free Barrett Brown. Dylan Harris likes Adrian Sanders's status. David Caddy likes Ian Brinton's status. Keith Armstrong likes Devos Krist's link on Gary Miller's Wall. Peter Robinson likes Luis Suarez. Jonathan Skinner likes GP Lainsbury's photo. Sean Bonney likes Jacob Bard-Rosenberg's link. Philip Nikolayev likes David Joseph Cribbin's note Shakespeare 450. Sophie Robinson likes Viral News. Tim Allen likes Tom Jenks's photo. Tamar Yoseloff likes Karen Dennison's link. Aidan Aodán McCardle likes Chiara Bautista's photo. Jeff Hilson likes Mandy Bloomfield's status. Pansy Maurer-Alvarez likes Cie Herman Diephuis's photo. Alan Baker likes Gregory Woods's status. Steve Dickison likes Duck Baker's link. Juha Virtanen likes Sean Bonney's post in London Poetry Festival. Michaela Ridgway likes Dorothy Lehane's post in Pighog Plus Poetry Night No 11. Eddy Odel likes Saturday Night Swing Club. Tim Barton likes Helen Drake's post in Photography & Music Event Bookbuster. Jesse Glass likes Archaeology Trowels and Tools's link. Jasper Brinton likes Peggy Hartzell's photo. Ellis Collins likes Booja-Booja. Susan Evans likes Paul McGrane's status. Erin Moure likes Jerome Fletcher's photo. Marcus Slease likes a photo on Tumblr. Tommy Peeps likes Richard B Smart's video music transcribed from where the birds are perching.

Text

Somebody is reading this text. Therefore it exists.

Thing

Well there's a thing. There's something to think about. Did you ever imagine such a thing? There's a whole thing here. What a thing to see. Would you credit it? That really is something. It's something to behold. There's something in it. Something you could never have imagined. But did you imagine it? Perhaps you did perhaps it was something in your imagination. Did this thing exist? Did it really exist? The thing is it was there and now it isn't. It was there and now it's gone. The thing is there was something there and it was really something but it's not there any more.

History of a thought

What is the history of thought? This is too hard a question. Try again. What is the history of a thought? Even more difficult. A thought is elusive. We know that much. Where did it come from? Unknown. A thought cannot be grasped. Its progress cannot be tracked with any certainty. Its genesis is therefore even less certain than its present status. What was there before the thought? If there was nothing how then did the thought originate? How could it originate? And what thereafter? How does the thought persist? Who is doing the thinking? How can we address this question? There is a narrative to a thought but it is too hard to capture. It mutates too quickly. It moves at the speed of thought. Tracking it is tricky even when it maintains its coherence. But what if it lost coherence? What if it went elsewhere? What if it became distorted and therefore entered the realm of dream or even nightmare? And what if it were then taken up and acted upon? That doesn't bear thinking about. But everything must run its course. Let us suppose therefore that before too long the thought is gone. It has vanished. Does the thinker then persist? Who is it who thought and then ceased thinking and does the thinker continue to exist after the thought has run its course? But has the thought really finished? Is it complete has it reached its terminus its estuary its final horizon? What has become of it? And if on the other hand still incomplete if without resolution then does the thought have a future and who will think it through? What is its future? We don't know. So we are no wiser. We don't even know that. This requires further thought. It's time to think again.

Be

That's it. What it is. That's what it is what it can be it is. What is it? That's what it is. What it is to be. What it is is to be. It is a name. It is to be a name. What can it be? Is what it is. And to be that. But there is no name. There is no name for it. No name for that. No name. That is if you need a name. That is if you need but what need is there? Is there and that's it. Is there. There is no need. You are there. You are there where it is. Just where it is. Where it is and what. Where is it? There it is. That's where it is. That's where you are. You are where it is where it all is. What it is what it all is is where you are. This is it. This is what it is. This is what you are. You are where you are and what you are. That is where it is and what it is. It's the same thing. Where it all is and what it all is that is where you are and all you are. Where it all can be and what it all can be that is all you can be. But just to be. That is all. Just to be that is all. To be and what it can be. What it can be to be. That's all it is. That's all there is to it. All that you can be is what it is. That's all. It is to be. Is that all? Is that all there is? To be it. To be. That's all there is. All there is. All there is is there. Is that it? Don't be frightened.

Breathe

Breathe in. Breathe out. Breathe in. Breathe out. Breathe in. And breathe out. Take it in. And let it out. Take it in. And let it out. Take it in take care. And let it all out. Take it in just take it in and take a break. And let it all come out just let it let it all come out. Take it all just take it take it all just take it all in. And let it out let it all out let it all come out. Take care take it in just take it all in just take it in and take a break. And let it out let it all come out it has to come out let it out. Take it in just take it all in just take care to take it all in just take it all just take it just take it all in then take a break. And let it out let it all out let it all come out it has to come out it's in there and it has to come out it has to come out somehow so just let it. Take care now just take care to just take it take care to take it in take care to just take it all in now this is the moment and take a break this is the moment. And gently start to let it out to let it out gently let it out with plenty of time the time is now to let it all out it's all in there and it's going to come out. Now this is the moment to take it in this is the right moment to take it in and take it all in and this is what happens in the moment in the right moment. And it's going to come out now it is now that it's out there it's out there out in the world now out in the world now out of this world and the time is now. So this is the right time to make a move and to move and to move to take everything in so everything comes in at the right moment with the right momentum. And out in the world the world moves it's moving now you can see how it is how it is now the clouds on the horizon how they are moving outwards how they are moving. So it moves in and in as the time is right and in and in and in time so everything moves in and it all moves in with the right momentum but there is no other. And back it goes with movement it has movement now the clouds on the horizon and the shadows of the clouds on the horizon as they move and move out of this world and move back and across the landscape moving out and back in the movement they have. There it is now it comes in when the time is right when they have plenty of time when they are sat on the lawn they are taking it all in the music is coming in from afar the music the sounds are coming into their ears and the time is right. And this gives it shape it takes the shape of the landscape that moves under the clouds you can see the landscape in motion now it has momentum it has no other shape but the shape its momentum gives it it is the momentum that gives it shape. Because the time is right there is no other time and it is right they are right to sit on the lawn in a circle and they are taking it all in and they find inspiration in it for that's what it is it's like a circle it is a circle. And the shape is the momentum the shape gives momentum and the momentum gives shape in the landscape under the clouds it takes shape the landscape in this moment that occurs. Because they are sitting in a circle or a half circle in the late sun in the waning sunshine they are taking it all in the music is coming in to their ears the music is a circle and they are half listening to the music which is an inspiration. And the landscape is a moment that occurs it takes shape it is gone it shapes and is gone its shape is a moment in time it is and was it was and is no more it responds and respires. It's like a circle it is a circle the music is a circle that is open they listen in the open they open their ears in a circle it's like a circle the music is inspiring it's like a circle it is an open book. And in a moment it's gone the moment has gone it takes shape and respires and the flame creeps in in the waning sun as it goes down the flame takes shape and it flares. It is a circle it's an open circle the music is a circle it is an open book you can go all round it and the circle surrounds it it is a circle of fire. And it respires and catches the flame catches in a moment it is a process of respiration it catches fire and takes and takes shape and takes and takes back. Then the fire takes hold the music is burning the books are burning in a circle of flame an open circle an open book in the fire that surrounds it. And takes and takes takes it back into the back where the shapes are where the human shapes are shuddering and they catch fire the bodies catch fire the human bodies are moving as they catch fire. So the fire moves into the open where the music the bodies the books are where they move and catch where they catch fire in a heartbeat two heartbeats three heartbeats four heartbeats. And so they are consumed the human shapes that shudder and move in the middle of four heartbeats they shout out loud in fear and joy. Then fear and joy consume them their bodies go up and down they shout in the midst of burning as the heartbeats race they shout the names of those they love. And love consumes them in the midst of it all all that burning they are burning creatures they are creatures of habit they are consumed by love as they burn so they burn so they do. Then fear and joy and bodies burning they are burning they shout the names. And burning creatures burn they are burning away and so they do. All the bodies will burn away and shout the names as they burn away. And so they do they burn and burn until there is nothing left and it comes to an end. They do it again and again once in every four heartbeats again and again they shout the names a million times two million times three million times four million. And soon it will come to an end even now it's coming to an end. The names they shout the names and soon the names are all that is left. And soon it will all be done and everything begins again. The names they call and soon the names they burn. And that's it you're nearly done. The names the burning names. And holding and burning and nearly done. Five hundred million times six hundred million. And soon and holding. Shouting the name of love. And holding and you're done that's it you're done. Do it seven hundred million times and you're done. And that's it you're done.

Time

Where were we? Let us begin. Once upon a time. But once there was no such time. No time as such. Everything was suspended. Everything was out of time we were not in time. We noticed that we were not in time. How is that that we were not in time that we were out of time? We're not in time we said. We noticed that it was noticed. Wait a minute we're not in time we said. Wait a minute. We were not in time at all where we were was where it was out of time or perhaps it was the deep time. Where it was was the deep time that was it the deep time. We were in deep. There was no time and yet it was said we had all the time in the world. Some said we were out of time and some said we were in deep time and some said that those were the days when we had all the time in the world. But we were out of our depth. They said we had all the time in the world. They said that. They said that time stood still. But you will recall they said that it would be moving that it would soon start to move. Then there was movement there was movement in deep time. Undoubtedly there was movement and it started to move. Then came movement like the tides solstices seasons like the cyclic motion of the heavenly bodies. Now they are moving. They are moving now in harmony the tides solstices seasons the heavenly bodies. They are moving now and they will always move. They will always move we said or that's what they said we said. That's what they said that it was natural movement. There is a circle in all other things that have a natural movement and coming into being and passing away. Time is a circle that's what they said and that's what we said. All other things are moving now and coming into being and passing away in time. Now we have all the time in the world we said or they said and we said it too. We have all the time we need. We can observe time moving that is to say objects moving through time and in time which is what time is. The incessant movement the rhythm and the beauty of mountains. The beauty of mountains and the moon and the tides that come and the tides that come and go. Did you see that we said did you see that? The tides and the mountains come and go. And we thought that they would come and go that they would come and go forever. And they come and go but they never repeat there is always a change there is no repetition they do not repeat they always change. There is no repetition in the way that they move in the way that they change. They are always changing what are they changing into? They are said to flow. Time flows they said. They are said to flow and so they do they flow and time flows and it flows on but it never flows back it doesn't go back it just goes where it's going all the time all the time it's flowing because if it didn't if it went back then it would go to the past and that's not where we're going the past is the time we're coming from which is the deep time or you might say the time spent but we're going towards what they call the future that's what they call the time time is flowing to the future which is the time that has not been spent the time that is waiting to be spent but where is it? And where are we in relation to it? Where are we now? Did you see that they said. What is it? We are waiting for the future but it never comes because we are waiting in time we can only wait in time time passes and the future never comes. Because the future isn't real because it isn't in time. They said the future isn't real only the flow is real but what is the flow what is it? What it is is time they said you can't stop time. You can't stop time they say but others say time must have a stop must time have a stop? Must time have a stop then? They say time is what stops. Time is what flows until it is spent and then it stops. Or they say time is an arrow. That is another thing they say. Time is an arrow it moves through the air they say it is pointing to where it is moving. There is a point to it. There is a point and it moves in the direction of the point. It moves through the air and when it reaches where it is going then it comes to a stop they say. The arrow points to the stop. That's the point. It must come to a stop. Time is what stops they say. Time is what stops. The arrow moves how does the arrow move? What is it that is moving? What is the point of it? The arrow moves through the air and the air moves past the arrow. Is it the air moving or the arrow? Time is moving but time is what stops everything. Everything must stop. Everything must stop one day they say. They believe that will happen. Time is what stops everything happening. Because everything is happening. Because everything is happening now but everything must come to a stop. Time is what stops everything happening at once. So they say. And so it happens and continues to happen one thing after another and this all happens over a long period of time. It happens and it happens one thing happens after another and it all happens in time. It's got to stop they say. Time after time it happens. Time after time after time after time it's all happening time after time. There is a lot happening and a lot to happen there is no time to lose. And if you want it to happen there is no time like the present. That's what they say. There's no time like the present. It's all happening you see the movement you see the rabbits hopping the rabbits stopping. It all happens very quickly you see the rabbits and the train coming out of the tunnel you go to school the teacher comes round with the biscuit tin going one or two one or two one or two you take three biscuits you get told off you soil your pants and come home crying your mother comforts you the church bells are ringing the choir sings all the family is there there are speeches there is a happy event and then there is another happy event and you have to move and things are not going well at work but that's how it all is how it all will be and it will all work out the boy is in Australia now the girl is going to get married it's all happening you had to move you have moved to a bungalow near the sea it's very nice you play tennis at the tennis club you play with the grandchildren everything's happening but starting to break down everything's breaking down it's not working like it used to in the past it's failing the prognosis is poor you have had a loss there can be no greater loss where has it all gone in this short time or this short space of time as they say this time we have we have time on our hands they say we weren't paying attention and suddenly it's all gone where has it gone when we weren't paying attention but there's no use dwelling in the past there's no time like the present that's what they say. But when everything stops happening then that means we're out of time your time's up they say. Your time's up mate. When everything that could happen has happened then we shall run out of time. The mountains will be levelled and the ice will melt and the moon and the tides and all that and the rabbits and all the little creatures therein that grow and flourish then die and become debris and everything then becomes debris and you become debris. That's a bit of a relief. It was fun while it lasted. But it's all too much please make it stop. So now we're out of time. Now we're running out of time. We don't have much time. We don't have much time left. How did that happen? We had all the time in the world but now it's almost gone it's almost spent it's almost a relief. There is not much time left. Time is up. We've spent the time. We've spent it all. Did we waste it? Did we waste time? Who knows? Time is running out there is not much time left now. Time is running out now. We're out of time. Our time is up. Time has run out. Now where were we?

Love story

He saw something. It was something and it was in her. In her there was a little smile. It was sudden and then it went. She danced and she smiled. There it went. There was dancing. She danced and he danced and she saw him. He was dancing too. Suddenly she saw him. He was running because it was late. He jumped the barrier and she saw him jumping. There was laughter. He saw her laughing. She laughed as he jumped. Then he laughed. There was something in it. There was recognition that was all. It was accomplished. It didn't take long. He saw something and she saw something it was something in her and something in him and it was the same thing. Many years passed. He still saw something in her and she in him. It was the same thing.

Who do you think you are

What is your name? What's your name? What's your name I can't answer that question. You can't answer that question no I can't I can't answer that question. Who are you? Can you say who you are who are you? Who are you that's a completely different question. You're right that is a completely different question. Can you answer that question? Can you answer the question I can't answer the question. I can't answer the question. Can't you remember? Can't you remember I can't. I can't remember. I can't remember the name or the who. What can you remember? I remember some things. Can you say what they are? There was a garden. There was a garden go on. Go on there was a garden. There was a garden I was a child. I was a child in a garden. What can you remember about it I was a child in a garden that's about it. Is that about it then is that all? Is that all that you can remember about it? Can you remember anything else? There were rabbits. There were rabbits that's good there were rabbits. Go on there were rabbits. Where were the rabbits they were in hutches. They were in hutches in rows and stacked on top of each other. Where were the hutches they were at the bottom of the garden and also at the side of the garden they were along two sides of the garden. Please continue. They were along two sides of the garden and there was a path and you could walk along the path and view the rabbits. Who did the rabbits belong to? No answer. Who did the garden belong to? No answer. Was it the garden of a house? No answer. Who did the house belong to? I was being taken to see my grandparents. Did the house belong to your grandparents? Did the house belong to your grandparents no it did not. What kind of a house was it? It was a boarding house my grandparents were staying in a boarding house I was being taken to see them and I saw them and then I saw the rabbits. How did you get there I don't remember. I was taken there. I was a child and I was taken to my grandparents. Were your grandparents kind to you I don't remember. Did your grandparents take care of you yes they took care of me. They took care of me. They took me for a walk. Where did they take you I don't remember. I don't remember. I remember I was a in a push chair. A push chair that's good. There was a bridge. I remember a bridge. Please continue. I remember a bridge my grandparents took me across the bridge. What kind of a bridge was it it was a pedestrian bridge. It was a pedestrian bridge across a railway track we stopped on the bridge. We stopped on the bridge in bright sunshine I was in my push chair and there was a noise. There was a noise in the bright sunshine. And there was a noise and the red thing came shooting out of the tunnel below us it came shooting out towards us below where we were on the bridge. My grandparents said look a train. Look they said here comes the train. I said that's not a train that's a tube. They said no it's a train look it's a train. I said no no it's not a train it's a tube. That's a tube. And I started to cry because they insisted it was a train. They insisted but I knew it was a tube I had been shown a tube before. I started to cry and they said all right it's a tube train it's a tube train that's what it is. And I said yes it's a tube train that's what it is. I began to stop crying they said it very gently they said it's a tube train we call it a tube train I said yes it's a tube train and that's about it. Can you remember any more? Can you remember any more no that's about it it was a tube train it came out of the tunnel and disappeared below us under the bridge and we never saw it again. That's about it. Is there anything more you can remember there is no answer. Is there anything more you would like to add there is no answer. What is your name there is no answer. Can you remember who you are there is no answer.

A death in the family

She's coming to fetch me tomorrow. Can you tell me what time? She's coming to fetch me. She's going to take us to the funeral. Who's died? She's going to fetch me she's coming to take us to the funeral. Who is it who died? It was my brother. My brother died. My brother died she's going to take us to the funeral. The bike isn't in the shed. She's coming tomorrow what time tomorrow? What time is she coming? I'm in a hell of a muddle you'll have to help me. That's tomorrow she's coming the funeral is tomorrow. What time is the funeral? I don't know. Twelve o'clock the funeral is at 12 o'clock. You'll have to excuse me who's died? My brother's died that's right. What time is the funeral 12 o'clock. When did he die? I don't know. What did he die of? I don't know. So tomorrow she's coming and then we're going to the funeral. She's coming and then we're going. That will be tomorrow. I had a little purse. We shall have to get ready that's right. What's happening tomorrow ah yes the funeral. We're going to the funeral tomorrow. You'll have to excuse me who is it we're burying? Ah yes my brother. The bicycle is no longer in the shed. Where can it be? What time do we have to get ready what time is this funeral? Ah yes 12 o'clock. We saw all the people arriving. The funeral is tomorrow who is it we're burying ah yes my brother. Do you know I am in a hell of a muddle. I used to have a little purse. She is coming to fetch me tomorrow I believe. That's right I believe she is. What time is she arriving? I don't know. When did he die? Two weeks ago. All the people were arriving. I don't know where it is. We shall have to get ready. Who was it ah yes my brother. What did he die of? Nobody knows. When did he die? Two weeks ago that's right. I don't know where my little purse is. It was quite sudden. She is going to fetch me and then we are going to the funeral. I remember my father called up the stairs are you up yet are you up yet in the way he used to do you know and he said get up come down here he said come down here you have a baby brother. And I told the man at the end of the road I had a baby brother and he said you'll be able to wheel him around in that little barrow of yours but I said I shan't wheel my baby brother around in a barrow. Do we have to get ready yet? What time's the funeral ah yes 12 o'clock. Do you remember? I can't say that I do. The funeral is in the church it is at 12 o'clock ah yes. Do you remember the funeral? You'll have to excuse me. Do you remember the horses? That's right. We saw the horses they were waiting outside. My brother gave me a little purse. It was the fourth of September 1942. I was being called up. My brother gave me his little purse but he waited until the very last moment and then he gave me his little purse he put it in my hand just as the train was moving off so I wouldn't have time to give it him back. That meant a lot to me. The bike is no longer in the shed. Maybe my brother would give me his bike or maybe I could buy his bike from him. Do you remember the funeral I can't say that I do. Ah yes that's right the funeral we saw the horses with their plumes. We were right behind the horses. We went through all the villages it was very peaceful. The sun came out. We went through all the villages. On the far side of the field we could see the other horses and they all had their coats on. It was very peaceful the sun came out. The sun shone on the villages and on the woods. We were right behind the horses with their plumes. And the other horses started cantering across the field towards us when they saw the horses. The other horses recognised the horses. Who were those people? I don't know. She's coming tomorrow. She's coming to fetch us what time was it tomorrow? Do you remember the funeral? I can't say that I do. You'll have to excuse me I'm in a hell of a muddle. Whose funeral was it? Ah yes at 12 o'clock the funeral is at 12 o'clock tomorrow.

Rest

How could it come to this? Who would have believed it would come to this? They had hoped it would come to nothing. What she had said came to mind. Her name came up at that time. What she had once said came to mind she had said that it wouldn't come to much. She had said it would all come to nothing. But then it all came to a head. By the time she said this everything had already come to a head and this is what came to light. So she was wrong it came to a head. That came to light pretty soon. It came to everyone's attention. Everyone came to the conclusion pretty soon that she had been wrong and they had been wrong because even then it was beginning to come to a boil. And people were beginning to come to conclusions about this. It all came out then. Things were coming apart. There was no coming back. Now things were coming to a close. People were beginning to come to terms with it. She wanted to come through but she couldn't. She just couldn't. She couldn't it just wasn't going to come out right. She came to realise this. She had come to the end of her tether. She came to a stop. She had come a long way she couldn't go on so she came to rest. She could go on no longer and so she came to rest. At last she came to rest. She is at rest now. She is at rest.

Black and white

Black is one and white are two. Two whites together black alone. One black and two whites all together and alone. The third white is nowhere to be seen. Two whites dance together. One black alone. The other black is nowhere to be seen. The sun is setting. The sun has set. There is no more light. There is no more to be seen.

Somewhere

We've got to go. We have to go. We've got to go we have to go in a minute. We've got to get going in a minute or so. There's a place we have to get to. We have to get to it wherever it is. That's the place. Wherever it is that's where we're going. Wherever it is we're going. It's been good. It's been good being here but now we have to go. There's a place to go. We have to go we're going now. We're starting off from here it's been good but now we're going. We have to find that place. That place is somewhere. We're going soon we have somewhere we need to get to. It's somewhere near here. It's around here somewhere. We're going somewhere we've never been before. We've been to many places but this is somewhere else. It's been hard going. We've been through all that but now we're getting somewhere. We're getting somewhere now at last at long last. We've been through a lot. We've been through a hell of a lot we've come a long way. But there is somewhere for us now it'll be good. It'll be good for us. It'll be good for the young ones. There is somewhere for the young ones. Somewhere good. The young ones will have somewhere to play. Somewhere there will be a place for them. Won't it be fun? It's somewhere quite close it's quite close by. There won't be any difficulty finding it. There it will be somewhere for everybody somewhere nearby. It's somewhere for everybody where everybody can find their own place. Somewhere there is a place. There's a place for everybody. We have to get there we have to find it there isn't much further to go now it's quite close we'll get there soon. We'll be there quite soon. Pretty soon we'll find it we'll be there. We're getting there. We're getting there any day now. Any day now we'll be there. It's somewhere else. We'll see you there.

Here and there

In there at first anywhere. When in in. How there then? When in on there more quickly. How out of into out of there? There from before before there there from before. More more quickly in at first then continuously. Continuously continually all together soon soon all together together all until as then. Then as of then by then like in at first in then continuously until like in all together continually. That together together alone. Then then of with of of with with then with with with then again how all together apart. Before there anywhere there anywhere for before. After over again never all together apart continually as of through. There there there. Here there there. After somewhere to somewhere for out of. In where to? Down here here how in? How there? That there there to. To then. Where to? Here. Here where from? From out of which across. To there there to. Across in along on to there. To at all of in out of there. How out of how here? Through without which which like which like which without without at first then continuously continually without when about. Where from out of anymore on where then? Where there where there about? Somewhere somewhere back then as in to forever anyway in to how. Where? About there. After all much at least not at all finally much about much there much there about. Then off then then beyond then through there beyond. After all. After all like much like really about. How really there? There there then there at least back back. Where about? About in there at least about there back there never back. Why? Where back? Why never back? Where back there? Here? Beyond from here into there then where? Where off? Here. Here there about what about? About where where how? Off where on where beyond where after where in upon whether as that in for into still there. In there beyond where then back through where where as much as when into there before into beyond into before in which into after into. There whether still about where. There here about here here in of where in all still there where in of. To where into for a while beyond left left to there then off then to right right again within about all around over then beyond where in for where until now.

Sound

There is no sound. There is no sound. Nobody is speaking. Nobody has spoken. Nobody has spoken for a very long time. There is nothing to be heard. Nothing. Not even a pin dropping. Not a pin. Dropping.

coda

Closure

I'm sorry we're closing. We'll be closing shortly. We will continue to be open for the next few minutes but then we are closing. We are shortly to close thank you. This is your final call. Thank you for everything. We'll be closing very soon now. It's nearly closing time now. Closing in a few minutes. Thank you. We are closing. Our closing time is in a few minutes from now. Please start to make your way to the exit. You have only a few minutes. Please make your way to the exit now. We're closing in the next few moments thank you. Please do not delay we're closing. Thank you we have to close now. The exit is this way. Please start to make your way out. Please make your way to the exit. We are now closing. Please make sure you have not left anything behind. We regret that we have to close now. This is the way out. The doors will be closing very soon. Please take extra care to ensure you have not left any personal belongings behind. Thank you for your patience. We're closing very shortly. Thank you very much. Please take care. We're closing imminently. Thank you and please take care as you go. Goodbye and thank you. I'm sorry we're now closed.

Lightning Source UK Ltd.
Milton Keynes UK
UKOW01f1106280816

281552UK00002B/29/P